D0938098

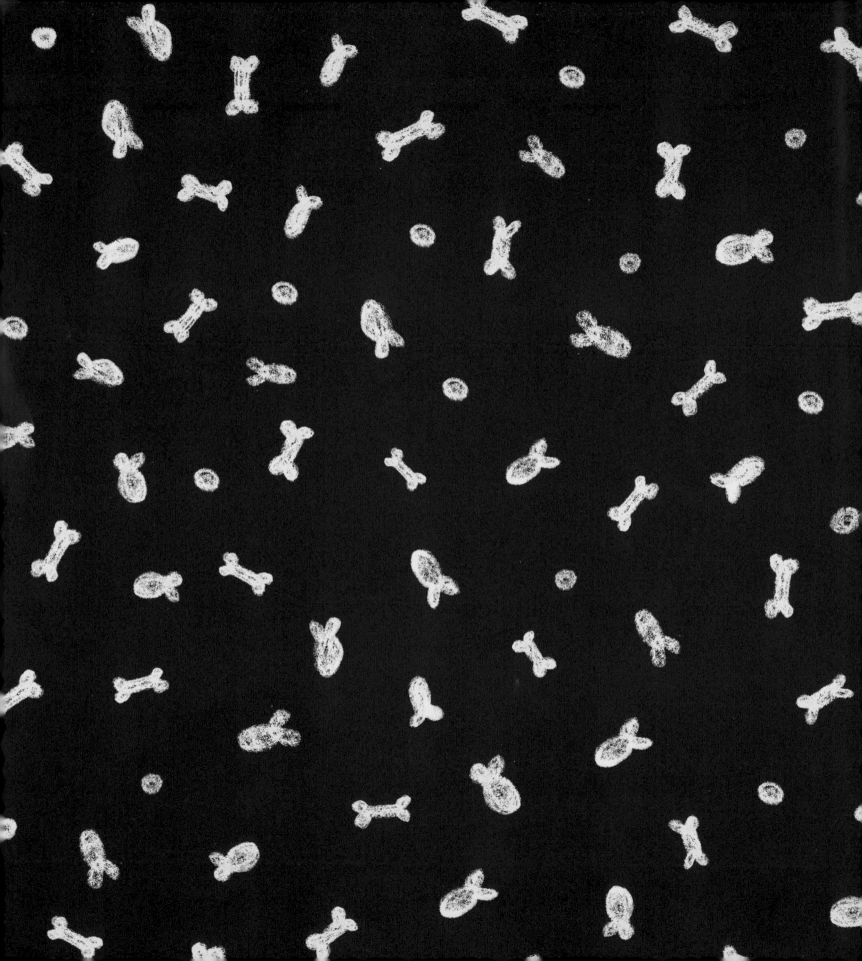

For the real "Fred"
Please don't ever do this again!

And to everyone else who helped with this book: Norm, Elisia, Katie, and David,
my eternal thanks—J.K.R

Clarion Books is an imprint of HarperCollins Publishers.

Lost Cat!
Copyright © 2023 by Jacqueline K. Rayner
All rights reserved. Manufactured in Italy. No part of this book may be used or reproduced in any manner
whatsoever without written permission except in the case of brief quotations embodied in critical articles and reviews.
For information address HarperCollins Children's Books, a division of HarperCollins Publishers,
195 Broadway, New York, NY 10007.
www.harpercollinschildrens.com

———————————————————————

ISBN 978-1-32-896720-6

———————————————————————

The artist used traditional media and digital collage to create the illustrations for this book.
Typography by Phil Caminiti
23 24 25 26 27 RTLO 10 9 8 7 6 5 4 3 2 1

First Edition

Rayner, Jacqueline K.,
Lost cat! /
[2023]
33305253953743
sa   05/04/23

LOST CAT!

JACQUELINE K. RAYNER

Clarion Books
An Imprint of HarperCollins*Publishers*

My cat, Fred, likes
butterflies, naps and cuddles
but mostly Fred likes food.

Last Thursday, when I called

him for dinner . . .

strangely, he did not come.

He wasn't hiding
under the bed ...

or snoozing on the sofa.

He
wasn't
in the
wardrobe,

in the garden ...

or at the neighbor's.

When he wasn't
back the next day,

I had
to find him!

My poor Fred . . .

Was he cold? Hungry? And all alone?!

Each day I called...

and searched...

and waited.
But as time passed ...

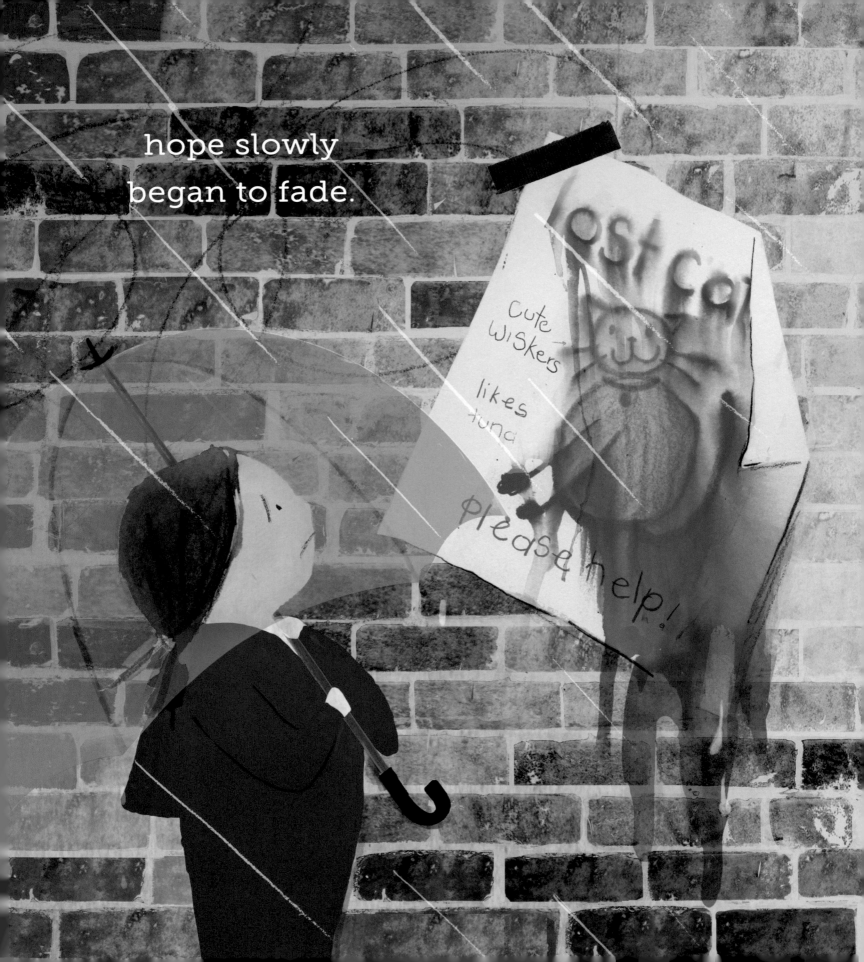

I'll never know where he went . . .

But just when hope was
all but lost...

He was finally
home!

Just in time for . . .

dinner.